Boogle
Bay

Look for these Just Right Books™

Just Right for 2's and 3's

MINE! A SESAME STREET BOOK ABOUT SHARING
By Linda Hayward
Illustrated by Norman Gorbaty

SALLY WANTS TO HELP
By Cindy Wheeler

Just Right for 3's and 4's

THE RUNAWAY CHRISTMAS TOY
By Linda Hayward
Illustrated by Ann Schweninger

SWEETIE AND PETIE
By Katharine Ross
Illustrated by Lisa McCue

Just Right for 4's and 5's

PATRICK AND TED RIDE THE TRAIN
By Geoffrey Hayes

THE CLEVER CARPENTER
By R. W. Alley

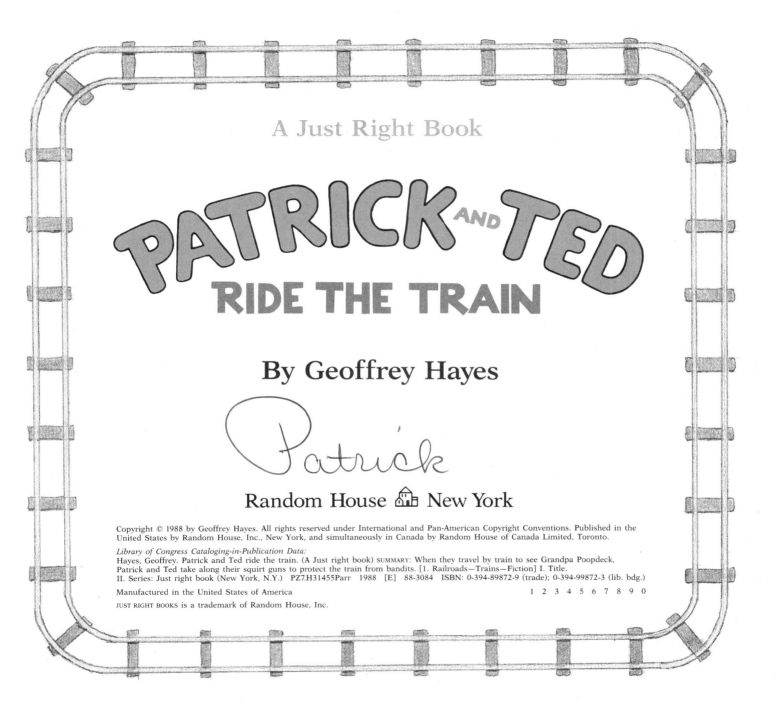

A Just Right Book

PATRICK AND TED
RIDE THE TRAIN

By Geoffrey Hayes

Patrick

Random House 🏠 New York

Copyright © 1988 by Geoffrey Hayes. All rights reserved under International and Pan-American Copyright Conventions. Published in the United States by Random House, Inc., New York, and simultaneously in Canada by Random House of Canada Limited, Toronto.

Library of Congress Cataloging-in-Publication Data:
Hayes, Geoffrey. Patrick and Ted ride the train. (A Just right book) SUMMARY: When they travel by train to see Grandpa Poopdeck, Patrick and Ted take along their squirt guns to protect the train from bandits. [1. Railroads—Trains—Fiction] I. Title. II. Series: Just right book (New York, N.Y.) PZ7.H31455Parr 1988 [E] 88-3084 ISBN: 0-394-89872-9 (trade); 0-394-99872-3 (lib. bdg.)

Manufactured in the United States of America   1 2 3 4 5 6 7 8 9 0

JUST RIGHT BOOKS is a trademark of Random House, Inc.

Mr. Willie the engineer and his partner, Yippy, had been working on the Scitter and Scoo since early morning. They had oiled the wheels, cleaned the smokestack, and polished the engine to a boot-black sheen.

As they finished, they saw Patrick, his friend Ted, and Mama Bear waiting at the station.

"Two tickets to Boogle Bay, please," said Mama Bear. "Patrick and Ted are spending the weekend there with Grandpa Poopdeck."

Mr. Willie sold Mama Bear the tickets.

"Will the train get to Boogle Bay by noon?" she asked.

Mr. Willie took a gold pocket watch from his trousers and snapped it open. "The Scitter and Scoo is always on schedule," he answered.

Yippy collected their tickets.

"Those are mighty fine squirt guns," he told Patrick and Ted.

"We're going to protect the train from bandits," said Ted.

"My, my," said Yippy.

He led them into the passenger coach. It was lined with rows of plush seats.

Patrick said, "Let's get one with a window."

"They all have windows," said Yippy.

Patrick and Ted waved good-bye to Mama Bear.
She gave them a loaf of corn bread for Captain
Poopdeck.

"Put this in the luggage rack," she said. "Be polite
to the other passengers, and remember to thank
Grandpa when you leave."

"We will," Patrick and Ted promised.

Mr. Willie hopped on the engine and pulled the whistle. "All aboard!" he hollered.

ALL ABOARD!

Yippy stoked the furnace with coal.
Huff! Huff! Clackety-clack! The little train sped down the track—out of the station and over a bridge.

And Mr. Willie and Yippy sang:

"Riding the rails,
We're riding the rails,
Bound for Boogle Bay!"

"Yay! What fun!" yelled Patrick and Ted.

"Are you boys old enough to travel by yourselves?" asked the lady in the next seat.

"Sure. We're cowboys!" cried Ted, waving his gun.

"Well, I hope you don't squirt that thing in here," she said.

Suddenly the train slowed down and stopped.

A Bleat was lying smack in the middle of the track.

"Move, you dumb animal!" barked Yippy.

Barking did no good. Neither did blowing the whistle.

"We need help," said Mr. Willie.

So everybody got off the train to help. They
pushed and they pulled, until finally the Bleat
decided to get up.

Mr. Willie checked his pocket watch.
"Holy moley! We've lost six minutes!" he said.
He raced back to the engine.

With an extra burst of speed, the Scitter and Scoo
wound through green fields, past houses and farms,
and into Pober's Wood.

"I'll bet there are bandits hiding in those trees,"
whispered Ted.

He and Patrick squirted their guns just in case.

The train stopped at Cow Junction so Yippy and
Mr. Willie could fill the engine with water.
Patrick and Ted filled their squirt guns from a
pump while a few new passengers got on.

Just as the train took off, Patrick and Ted saw two weasels climb aboard the caboose.

"It's Jiminy and Biminy Bingo!" Patrick cried.

Mr. Willie came by, collecting tickets. "What's up?" he asked.

"There are bandits on the caboose," Ted told him.

Mr. Willie opened the door. A weasel tail was hanging over the roof of the caboose.

"Hee, hee, hee! We ride for free!" sang Jiminy and Biminy.

"Come down from there this instant!" called Mr. Willie.

Just then the train came to a tunnel.

Jiminy snickered. "I see a way to have a bit of fun, Brother Biminy."

He leaped to the roof of the passenger coach and then crawled through a window. So did Biminy.

The weasels ran down the aisle, screaming like ghosts and knocking people's hats off.

When the train came out of the tunnel, they were in the luggage rack.

"I smell corn bread," said Jiminy, grabbing Mama Bear's package.

"Let's stop for lunch!" cried Biminy. He pulled the emergency cord.

Yippy slammed on the brakes, and the Scitter and
Scoo screeched to a halt.
Everyone fell on the floor in a heap.

Jiminy and Biminy jumped out the window with the corn bread.

"Oh, no you don't!" cried Patrick.

He shot Jiminy in the pants with his squirt gun. Jiminy squeaked and dropped the corn bread.

"Good shot!" said Ted.

Mr. Willie grabbed the weasels by their suspenders.

"You troublemakers have made us lose *four* more minutes," he said.

"Are we going to be late?" asked Patrick.

"No. We can make up the time," said Mr. Willie. "I'll put Jiminy and Biminy to work shoveling coal."

The Scitter and Scoo took off like lightning. It clattered up and down hills, through a summer shower, and rolled into Boogle Bay at twelve noon on the dot!

"The Scitter and Scoo is always on schedule," said Mr. Willie.

Captain Poopdeck was there to greet them.
"Guess what, Grandpa?" Patrick cried. "We helped save the train from bandits!"

Mr. Willie let Jiminy and Biminy go.

"Remember, there are no free rides," he told them.

The two engineers got ready for their return trip to Puttyville. Captain Poopdeck gave each of them a piece of corn bread to eat on the way.

Soon the Scitter and Scoo was chugging down the
tracks once more. And Patrick and Ted could hear
Mr. Willie and Yippy singing:

"Riding the rails,
We're riding the rails,
Home from Boogle Bay!"